The plunge of death

The Plunge of Death

Francis Kiarie

Published by Francis Kiarie, 2024.

The plunge of death

This is a work of fiction. Similarities to real people, places, or events are entirely coincidental.

THE PLUNGE OF DEATH

First edition. October 30, 2024.

Copyright © 2024 Francis Kiarie.

ISBN: 979-8227108340

Written by Francis Kiarie.

Dedications

I dedicate this book to all my family members both in Kenya and in the USA.

May the lord bless us, protect us from all evil and bring us to everlasting life. Amen.

TABLE OF CONTENTS

Before conversion

Chapters 1 – 15

After conversion

Chapters 16 - 19

Introduction

Influenced by the love he saw between his parents and some of his married friends, Jack Karaya desired to get married immediately after graduating from university and getting a job. He thought marriage was the magic pill for happiness. Notwithstanding his education, his myopic eyes could not see a vast multitude of married couples whose lives were far from being happy.

Being the first-born he assumed that he must win in all situations. His pride did not entertain the idea of losing or rejection and when it happened it left him gravely wounded emotionally.

And so believing that success depended on his effort he worked very hard. His industry enabled him to get a good job and his employer had no problem with him and even liked him.

He related well with other people and had a small circle of friends, some of whom were married. The latter appeared a happy lot and he attributed their happiness as a result of their being married. This inspired him to get married, unfortunately, the few women he fell in love with left him wounded and in grief. When he had finally given up on marriage, he met by chance a stunning half-caste beauty and both of them fell in love with each other at first sight.

He always looked on the outside of a woman, never the inside. The wise men throughout the ages have always stipulated that all that glitters is not gold.

This story then, is about what happened to Jack after meeting this woman he thought was his soulmate.

One

One would not be grossly mistaken to conclude that Jack Karaya might not have met, one Claudia Mills, had it not been through the intermediary of Mercy Murugi, popularly known by her friends, and her foes as Double M.

For three years, Jack, aged 26 had been working in the coastal city of Mombasa, having been born and raised in the upcountry city of Nairobi. He was tall, slender, and of dark complexion. At school, he had been nicknamed 'Makena' meaning the 'happy one ' for he had a smile for everyone, and as a rule, he always wore a neat short beard. Similarly, as a rule, he had a line parting his hair on the left side of his face.

Mercy, on the other hand, was the girlfriend of one of Jack's small circle of close friends, some of whom he had met at the University. She was fond of Jack in a brotherly sort of way, probably because they hailed from the same area, or perhaps for any other mysterious reason, unknown even to her. She had a gap between her front teeth and was always full of laughter and a hug for everyone. She liked to talk and always dominated any gathering she was in. So, as might be expected, some people liked her and others detested her.

And so one day when Jack was busy at work, he received a phone call. He immediately recognized Mercy's voice. "Hello Double-M, long time no hear," he said into the mouthpiece, his voice betraying his surprise.

"Hello Jack," she said with an unmistakable joy to hear Jack's voice. "How are you?"

"I am surviving, Mercy. What is up? I am missing you a lot." He said, infected by her joyful voice.

"We too, Jack," she said breathlessly, "however, you're ever in our minds, notwithstanding the distance."

"So am I," he said.

"However, I am calling to bother you a little, my brother." She said expectantly.

"What are friends for, Double-M, if not to lean on each other 's shoulder?"

He said, even though he was unsure what it was all about.

"Exactly. Let me get to the point," she said pausing a little for breath.

"Please go ahead," he said and patiently waited.

"There is a young lady from our office who is being transferred to Mombasa." She paused a little to allow him to get the picture, then continued: "She doesn't know the city or anyone there." Again another brief pause. "I am therefore requesting you to let me know whether you can be a spot and show her around."

Her message was brief and clear.

Jack hesitated briefly, wondering what kind of request that was. Did Double-M have an ulterior motive, like perhaps introducing her to him, albeit clandestinely? He did not wish to waste his time conducting a boring female around the city.

However, to Double-M he said: "Anything for you Double-M, as long as she isn't somebody else 's wife."

"Thanks, Jack. I knew l could count on you. Have no fear bro, l can never put you into Jeopardy." Double-M assured him and hung up the phone.

Jack thought: Are human beings any different from animals, seeking security from their kind? It started from the beginning. Even Adam could not get a life partner from a different species of created beings. God created for him his kind.

Due to the pressure of work at the factory, where he worked as an engineer, he completely forgot about that call until two weeks later when he received another call. The voice was of a woman he could not recognize. "Hello," he said into the mouthpiece, "this is Jack Karaya. What can I do for you?"

"My name is Claudia Mills," the voice said. "I am a colleague of Double-M. She told me she had spoken to you about me."

Her voice did not sound the sophisticated hic urban type, that Jack preferred for company. However, you cannot judge a book by its cover, and so into the mouthpiece, he said: "Oh yes she did. Now I remember. Forgive my creaky memory. Have you been here long?"

"It is two days now." She said.

"Where are you staying?" he asked.

"I am staying at the YWCA hostel," she said in a relieved voice.

"Can I pick you up there on Saturday?" he asked.

"Yes, if I shall not be bothering you."

"No, you will not be bothering me at all. It will be my pleasure," he said with faked enthusiasm.

Two

However, one day before the appointed Saturday, the lady named Mary Njoki, whom Jack had been pursuing very passionately lately called him. The way he met her was itself very fascinating. He had been to a social place with two married friends, when a very pretty woman passed by their table, on her way to the restroom. The two married friends noticed how Jack's eyes followed the woman to the restroom. One of his friends who had bulging eyes like a frog, and whose name was Fred, said to him wryly: " Why don't you get her Jack?"

"What do you mean?" Jack said, embarrassed, for having been caught red-handed snooping, as though he had been caught in the act of raping her.

"Just what I have said," he insisted, still grinning, but not backing down.

"You cannot hide your interest in her Jack. It is written all over your face." The other friend added, also with a wide grin. His name was Tom, and he had big ears like a rat. It intrigued Jack why the two were inseparable, like parts of one body, and seemed to miss nothing of what went on in the small city.

Jack said, submitting: "You can't deny she is beautiful. Who is not attracted by such beauty, even you two? However, I notice she is sitting with a guy at the counter, who might be her husband or boyfriend."

Their eyes turned to the counter, where the man, now alone, was sitting smoking a cigarette pensively.

Fred said: "Oh, you need not worry about the man. His name is Peter, and he operates a filling station on the western side of the city. Besides, he is married."

Jack felt relieved, the two appeared to be encouraging him, not rebuking him. He did not ask himself questions, starting with why she should be with a married man at a social place. He was concerned only with her beauty.

"Is there anyone you two don't know in this city?" Jack said in loud laughter, "Both of you are perfect candidates for electoral positions."

Before any of his friends could respond to his remarks, the pretty lady re-emerged from the restroom. Tom, who was sitting on his right stepped hard on one of his boots under the table and said jovially. "Here she comes, lover boy. Brace yourself like a man and speak to her. I will tell you her name. She is called Mary Njoki and works at one of the tourist' hotel on the north coast. Show us the stuff you are made of, or forever be silent."

The gauntlet was thrown at his feet. It was as though they were challenging him to prove to them he was a worthy companion to them, who in their opinion were real men.

Eager to accept the challenge, he took a deep breath when she approached their table, in a cooing voice, which amused the two friends he said to her, " Hello Mary. Why don't you join us and spruce our table with your feminine presence?"

Beyond Jack's expectation, she stopped by their table, smiling sweetly at them.

"I am Jack," he said, "and here is Tom, and here is Fred."

The two friends nodded their heads invitingly. She responded with a smile replete with charm.

She said: "I am pleased to meet you, gentlemen. My name is Mary Njoki."

"Please sit down," said Jack rising to get an extra chair from the next table.

She stopped him with her hand saying: "I would love to join you gentlemen, but I am with someone else at the counter. Perhaps some other time."

"Won't you join us even if for only one beer?" Jack pleaded with her.

"Let it be another time, sweetheart," Mary said getting on her way elegantly, to join her companion.

No, she had not rebuffed them. She had only been courteous, Jack thought.

The two friends looked at Jack favourably. The one called Fred said: "Don't relent. You shall get her."

Tom agreed with him by giving him a big smile.

Jack rejoiced because he had not let down his friends. He did not realize he ought not to have given a hoot to whatever opinion they thought of him. They were fellow human beings. The judgment that matters is that of God who created and cares for him. For all he knew his friends might be leading him to a very big mistake.

Jack admired his married friends. They seemed to have everything sown up. They seemed contented with their lives, and that is what he wanted for his own life. That was the genesis for his hunger to get married, and live a contented life. He attributed their contentment to being married.

He took his friend's advice to heart and the following day he called Mary at her office. She was receptive and they started dating. He wanted to get her, to prove to his friends he was someone to be reckoned with, and not someone to hold in derision.

"Sweetheart," she called, the day before his planned outing with Claudia. "I have a friend who has been admitted to the hospital. Would you please take me to see her tomorrow?"

What is happening? How about Claudia? Jack thought. He felt he was in a tight spot. However, he knew he could never let Mary down. His relationship with her was just beginning. He could not risk turning down her request for fear of losing her. A bird in hand is worth two in the bush, he reasoned.

"What time?" He asked her.

"Please pick me up at around ten in the morning." She said, pleased he had agreed.

So on that Saturday morning, instead of going to pick up Claudia, he went to pick up Mary. One woman for another. Better a devil you know than an angel you don't know.

Three

When he went to pick up Mary, he found her with another lady. She was dark in complexion, and the black dress seemed to enhance her darkness. She was a bit shorter than Mary but heavier.

"This is Susan," Mary told him. "She is my friend, accompanying me to visit our friend."

"I'm pleased to meet you, Susan," Jack said smiling and offered his hand to her.

"I'm pleased too Jack," she responded shaking his hand. She appeared like he had met her before but he could not pinpoint where.

Signs that this would be a bad day for Jack started to manifest themselves even before the journey began. When he opened the car doors for them they chose to sit at the back seat together. He would have preferred for Many to sit beside him in the front seat so that he could chat with her on the way to cement their relationship. He thought perhaps in her grief she wanted to seek comfort from her female companion, which would be perfectly in order. And so he unhappily accepted the situation.

The journey to the distant hospital was to take them about two hours. To his consternation, the two females turned out to be chatterboxes. To his annoyance, he did not know what they were talking about so animatedly. Sometimes they laughed hilariously without any hint of sadness, as though their sick friend was far from their minds. It was as though they were attending a party. It irritated Jack, causing him to drive too fast so that halfway through the journey he was flagged down by a traffic policeman, whose car was hidden in the bush he could not see. As the policeman approached him his ticket book in one hand and a walkie-talkie in the other, he said: "How are you Honorable? Is it a car you are driving or an aeroplane you are flying?"

"I am sorry," said Jack apologetically.

The officer went around Jack's car to look for any visible defects, then said to him: "May I have your driving license."

Jack knew the drill too well and got out of the car. He pretended to hand him his driving license, but in his hand was a five hundred shillings note. In a low voice, the officer said: "It is not enough. In court, you will be fined five thousand. At least give me half of that."

"That's all I have," replied Jack. "I am rushing a sick person to the hospital, and I am afraid she may die if I delay much longer."

The policeman looked hard at him to ascertain whether he was lying then said: "Go, and from here drive slowly, you don't want to kill your patient as well as yourself."

"Of course not." He said glumly

He returned to the car furious, but for the rest of the journey, he drove slowly.

On arrival at the hospital he parked his car at the parking lot, and turning to Mary said: "You may go and see your friend, I will wait for you in the car."

"Don't you want to see the patient?"

"What is the point? She doesn't know me, nor do I know her."

"We will try not to take too long," said Mary not ready to persuade him too much. She noticed that he was moody, but did not know why.

"You can take as long as you want," Jack responded indifferently.

When the two got out of the car, he had a strong urge to drive off and abandon the two there, but after some soul-searching, he relented shut the windows reclined his seat, and dozed off, because he was tired.

Four

He fell asleep almost immediately. He was woken up by a gentle tapping on the window glass when the two returned about three-quarters of an hour later. He said: "You are back too soon." He had not realized how long he had slept

"We thought we might keep you waiting too long," said Mary.

"Never mind that. You did not come here because of me. How is the patient?"

"She is much better. She will be discharged in a day or two."

"That is very good," he said raising his seat. "Can we now go home?"

"Yes," answered Mary.

The two chatterboxes were back at it again when they re-entered the car and Jack drove off. Their mouths seemed to have been recharged. It was as though he was ferrying two parrots. It almost drove him crazy. To occupy himself he decided to observe the scenery as he drove by. It was a brilliant idea for he was amazed by the beauty he saw everywhere. He wondered what was in God's mind when he created all of that. He saw what he had not seen, not because it had not been there, but because he had not bothered to look. No wonder Scripture says: Seek and you shall find. He saw trees big and small of various types. Some were fruit trees, others just ordinary trees that could be used for various purposes. They were the homes for birds of various types, and apart from beautifying the landscape, they attracted rain. He saw bushes and shrubs, that were food and shelter to animals. He wondered if was green God's favourite colour? No, among the grass he saw flowers of myriad hues. He spotted hills and gullies and borders jutting their ugly heads like people resurrecting from the dead.

He drove at a snail's pace to observe all that. Ah! It was beautiful. If the traffic cop who had flagged him down earlier, happened to spot him now, he would have had nothing to complain about, perhaps only regret the missed opportunity to coax a bribe from him.

If his companions in the back seat, who chatted non-stop detected any change in him they gave no indication. They were wrapped in a world of their own beyond the reach of Jack. They did not notice him or what he was gazing at. For the first time, he was amazed at God's creation. He thought of the universe, the sea, and everything therein. Everything was beautiful. He glanced at the two chatterboxes behind, to see if he could discern any beauty in them. Perhaps only with a magnifying glass could you discover any beauty in them. Their disregard for him had obscured any beauty they may have had. The anger in his heart had clouded his eyes. His pride had been wounded.

And so distracted by the pleasant meadows through which they were passing, he forgot where they were going until he found himself at the parking lot of the hotel where he first met Mary. He felt thirsty and hungry, but more than physical thirst and hunger, he was thirsty and hungry for Mary's attention.

"Oh, we are at the Splendid Hotel!" The chatterboxes exclaimed happily. "How
quickly time has flown."

It was with much effort that he restrained himself from slapping them.

Five

As the two stepped out of the car and proceeded to the hotel entrance, he remained behind locking the car. He watched them hurry to the hotel and wondered whether he should follow them to incur further expenses. How much is much? However, drawing from his store of resilience he followed them to find out and found them sitting on one side of the table, implying he should sit on the other side. This was too much. Even here he would have no opportunity to whisper something into Mary's ear.

He ordered a drink and they ordered theirs. He promptly paid the bills, his body language indicating he would pay no more bills. They drank in suffocating silence.

After finishing his drink, he assessed the situation, and turning to Mary said: "I want to leave. Are you coming with me?"

"It is too early to go home, Jack," Mary said.

"I am tired. I want to go home and rest," said Jack stiffly.

Mary glanced at Susan as though to seek her opinion. Noting only a blank expression, she said to Jack flatly; "You may go. It is too early for us."

"Don't you want me to drop you at your house?" He pursued hoping for a chance to be alone with her.

"We will make it on our own," said Mary ungratefully, insensitive to his needs.

As he rose from his seat he nodded at Susan. She tried to smile but it came out crooked.

And that was how they repaid him for transporting them to visit their sick friend - a kick in his bottom. His feet felt as heavy as lead as he departed in anguish. Not only had he wasted his time and money, but had allowed himself to be made a fool of. He truly felt sorry for himself.

What Jack was not aware of was that all that happened was a machination of Susan. They had indeed met before, and while she had deeply fallen in love with him, he had not paid her the slightest attention. He did not notice her, so to speak, even though she tried to make him notice her. She felt hurt and slighted by his indifference towards her. When she learned he was dating her friend, Mary, she swore to herself that she would try to thwart their relationship. She had the evil spirit of a vandal who destroys something to stop anyone else from having it. The opportunity came to fruition when she learned he was taking Mary to visit their sick friend. She insisted that she accompany them. Mary could not be happier. Naive Mary, could not discern that Susan was bent to ensure she never had any moment to talk to Jack. And in her ingenuity correctly predicted the outcome. If she could not get him, Susan swore, she would not allow anyone she knew to have him.

And so as Jack left them behind seated contentedly, he walked wobbly, his head stooped for shame and his shoulders hunched, resolved never to see Mary again.

And as Susan watched Jack leave, his face contorted with pain, her own heart purred for joy, as that of a cat lapping milk in a bowl. Oh, how fickle human friendship can be? Mary thought Susan was her best friend while she was not, for she thought only of herself, and blocked others from achieving what she could not. Envious, she celebrated wrecking the relationship between Jack and Mary. She was truly a wolf in sheep's clothing, and she was smart enough like all conmen, for neither Jack nor Mary got the vaguest clue of what she had deftly accomplished.

Six

At home, Jack prepared himself a snack and went straight to bed even though the sun had not yet set. He did not switch on his music as was his custom. The silence in his house was deafening, as though he was mourning. Yet, even though tired, sleep could not come to his eyes. The events of that day bombarded his mind. To purge out the memory of the day, he thought of Claudia. She must have been very disappointed when he failed to turn up and pick her up, he thought. He ought to have been courteous to at least postpone the appointment, but Mary's request had not given him time to do that and until today, she took first place in his scheme of things. Claudia might have prepared herself thoroughly in the manner of women only to be so disappointed. What a coincidence that both Jack and Claudia will sleep that night in deep disappointment. At least it was a payback for him. Probably if Claudia had known that, she might have felt much relieved. It is our broken human nature to rejoice when things turn out awry for someone who has let us down. Tit for tat, we often call it. Fate handed Jack the measure he had given.

The following day was a Sunday, but he quit attending church a long time ago. He thought the church was for people who had failed in life. He wanted nothing to do with failures. For him, the successful people whom he embraced were those people with possessions, those with status, and the famous. He thought they were smart people and he longed to emulate them. Even with his education, it had not dawned on him that we come into this world with nothing, and similarly leave it with nothing, and that whatever we acquire is merely a gift from God, to share with those not similarly gifted. In his myopic eyes, he had not observed that the rich are not always the happiest people.

At school, and even at the University he had joined the choir, but that was simply because he loved singing and music in general, and could play several musical instruments. Music, then was the only reason that could make him enter a church.

However, apart from attending weddings and funerals, he no longer attended church. He was an avid reader of books and had come across some books written by renowned atheists, who had put some doubts in his mind of the existence of God. He thought their arguments were plausible. Still, it is not clear why he had not been convinced by the more renowned apologists, who demonstrated the existence of God. Could it be the power of Satan that had darkened his mind to hinder him from seeing the light of the world, who is Jesus himself, and get saved?

Oddly enough there were times he had welcomed in his house roving preachers, who after leaving found him considering changing the way he lived, which meant stopping drinking and chasing women. However, a day or two later all of that would be forgotten. His had been the seed that fell by the roadside, as the sower sowed and got eaten by the birds. He too easily gave in to temptations, like our first parents.

So on this Sunday, he lingered long in his bed, debating with himself whether to go check on Claudia, or not to go. When he could not sleep, he left the bed and lay on the couch, in the living room and continued with the debate. Finally, at around midday, feeling restless, he decided he had nothing to lose, and drove to Claudia's hostel.

"Good afternoon," he said to the receptionist upon arrival.

"Good afternoon to you," she said sweetly to him, revealing even white teeth. She was fairly young, very smartly dressed, and had respectfully put down a document before her.

"I would like to see one of the residents by the name Claudia Mills if she is around," he said nervously.

She pointed at a chair before her and said: "If you may sit there, I will go and fetch her for you."

"Yes please," he said returning her smile with one of his own. However, his teeth were not as white as hers, because of his unfortunate habit of smoking.

Seven

As he waited for Claudia to come, he was in deep thought figuring out how to explain to her why he had failed to show up yesterday. He was searching his mind for a plausible explanation when after a short time the receptionist returned accompanied by a tall slender half-cast woman, a far cry from what he had imagined. Her voice on the phone had belied her stunning looks. He was a shy fellow, especially before beautiful women, and so he stammered a little when he said: "Hello, I am Jack Karaya. I presume you are Claudia Mills."

She noticed his shyness, but she was accustomed to that, especially among the men she met for the first time, and thought it was normal.

"Yes I am Claudia and I am very pleased to meet you, Jack." She said truthfully.

It was the voice he had heard over the phone, but face to face with her, it sounded so melodious, so different.

He said to her: "I have come to apologize for my failure to turn up yesterday as we had arranged." He stammered some more in confusion, as he searched in his mind for a plausible explanation. He hated telling lies, for truth always sets us free, but how could he tell her what happened yesterday? The truth must remain buried forever in

this case. So he told her: "I meant to come, but something happened at work, and I had to attend to it. By the time we had sorted out the problem it was too late, and I was tired."

As he spoke, she was keenly studying him. She noticed he was as tall as she was, not much older than her, and his appearance was agreeable. She said: "I am sorry you had a problem at the factory. Your work should come first. I understand why you failed to come."

Nothing could have pleased him more than what she said. It was music to his ears. Nonetheless, his keen eyes observed that the young receptionist was eavesdropping on their discussion, so to prevent it he led Claudia out to the parking lot where he had parked his car. It was a beautiful car that raised his status in Claudia's eyes. They sat on the bonnet as he said: "If it's fine with you I could still take you out today. She looked excited as she said: "I have nothing planned for today so if I will not be inconveniencing you we can go."

"No, you will not be inconveniencing me in any way," he said enthusiastically.

"Then allow me a minute to go and change," she said.

As she went to change, he suddenly realized he did not have enough money. What shall I do? He asked himself in panic. What had he got himself into? It was something he had not thought about before leaving the house. He had been nursing the wounds suffered yesterday to the extent that he could not think straight about today, which was what mattered for yesterday was gone and dusted. Still, his car had enough petrol, maybe it might do to drive around the town and its environs, and in the process get to know her better. However, his desire to impress her could not allow him to enjoy her company.

Eight

He was still pondering what to do when she returned. It had not taken her long to change. She came wearing gray jeans, a cream long-sleeved blouse, and white sports shoes. She looked stunning, leaving him confused. He opened the car door for her as though she was a celebrity. It was only when she was properly settled, after adjusting her seat to give room for her long legs did he get into his driving seat.

"Are you comfortable?" He asked her like a mindful guide. She sat beside him arousing the bitter memory of yesterday.

"Yes I am, thanks." She responded her face showing satisfaction.

She liked his car. It was sleek and neat, but most of all she liked him. Not only was he handsome, and very considerate, but he looked the type who knew how to treat a woman like a lady. She was barely twenty, yet she had a mature woman's intuition.

⸻ ◉ ⸻

WHEN SHE HAD BEEN PICKED from her office to be transferred to Mombasa, Double - M had asked her: "Are you thrilled to be transferred to Mombasa?'

"Should I be?" She had asked curiously.

"I would be if I were you. First of all, it is an opportunity to get away from the hustle and bustle of this awful city."

"Is it any different in Mombasa?" She had asked attentively.

"A lot different, Claudia," Double - M asserted authoritatively. "Life there is easygoing in a sleepy kind of way. People there are kinder and not as it is the case here, where you have to be ever alert lest someone cut your throat."

"It sounds like paradise then," Claudia said smiling with relief.

"Double - M said: "For a long time it had been so, until the criminal types from here invaded there, mudding the waters of peace there, although it is yet to reach the level it is here."

Claudia said: "Even though I have not travelled much, I think it's the same everywhere, for people are basically the same. There are some peaceful cities and others full of criminals."

Double - M agreed saying: "Yes, it seems like there are some places that are attractive to criminals and others that are not. Probably it has to do with the strictness and laxity of the administration of justice in those areas."

"Since you seem to like Mombasa that much, why don't we change places, you go and I remain here?" Claudia said smiling.

"It is your good luck, you go and I remain, but I know someone who can take care of you there," Double -M continued." If you wish I can introduce you to him."

"You mean someone like a tour guide?"

"Sort of except it would be free." Double - M said teasingly.

"I am scared of free offers. Sometimes they end up being very expensive."

"What is the matter girl? I can never put you up to any risk. This person can't even hurt a fly." Double -M said confidently.

"In that case, there is no harm in trying," Claudia accepted the offer with a radiant smile.

"That is my Claudia. Ever careful," said Double -M with a grin that extended from one ear to the other, as she wrote down a name and a telephone number on a piece of paper and handed it to Claudia.

***

ON SETTLING DOWN IN the car, she vividly recalled that conversation as she carefully studied Jack's every move, at the beginning of their outing. Jack had no idea what was going on in her mind.

Jack switched on the stereo system and soft music filled the car. It was like being in a music hall. It made both of them relax as he drove around town pointing to her the various features of interest. Sometimes he would stop the car and explain to her in detail the unique features of the town, and then they would resume. By the time they had covered the whole of Mombasa, it was as though they had known each other all their lives. It seemed to her that what Double - M had said about him was true.

She felt no inhibitions whatsoever when she answered some of his subtle questions about herself and her likes and dislikes.

At the back of each other's minds, truth be told, their main interest was not so much as to see the town, but to see each other - to get to know each other. For Jack, he wanted to spend every minute of the afternoon with her in the cheapest possible way.

And so when they had seen almost everything in town, which he thought was worthy seeing, and mindful of his pocket, and the afternoon was still young Jack ingeniously decided to kill more time by crossing to the mainland where the factory he worked in was located.

Nine

Since it was on a Sunday, there were not very many people at the factory, except those who were working on shift. He had a key to his office, and he took her there where they drank cold water from a water fountain. Then he slowly conducted her on a tour of the factory, finally taking her in a lift to the highest tower from where they could see, as though in a helicopter all of Mombasa and its environs. They viewed the whole expanse of the ocean, as far away as their eyes could see, and saw ships, small and big, entering and leaving the harbour. They could see every scenery on the island, and the view was breathtaking. They saw all the roads and their traffic, leaving and entering the island, like the arteries of the body circulating the blood, but try as she could, Claudia could not locate her hostel, for it was just a minuscule dot from this distance. Up above them, they saw a vulture that effortlessly floated in the air. Its keen eyes seemed to observe them, probably curious about what they were doing there. It might have observed such incidents many times before - people viewing the area from the tower. Or probably drawn by its hunger, it thought they wanted to jump. Hunger can make even human beings see food where there is not any. It is what is called a mirage. The vulture waited long enough but when they failed to jump, it flew away in search of any carrion elsewhere to gorge on.

"You are not afraid of heights?" Jack said smugly.

"Not really," she replied, her voice lacking confidence.

Jack nudged himself close to her and with his shoulder pretended to push her.

Taking his cue, she said laughing: "I have changed my mind."

They both burst into hilarious laughter.

While at the tower, for our minds are never still, Jack reflected on Satan's temptation of Jesus, when he took him to the pinnacle of the temple, showed him all of his kingdom, and asked him to fall to his knees and worship him, so that Satan may give Jesus all he had shown him. Although Jesus had neither eaten nor drank anything for forty days and was truly famished he declined the offer. And yet he, who was neither hungry nor thirsty even for a day, wondered what he could offer Claudia to be all his. He could have gladly fallen to his knees and worshiped her if that had been her request. Jesus stood up to Satan, while ignorant Jack embraced him. Still, he sensed, for there are things that cannot be hidden, that Claudia liked him but he wanted to tread carefully. He did not want to scare the bird before he had a proper grip on it.

⸺⬤⸺

SATISFIED HAT CLAUDIA had seen enough of the factory, and noting what was left of the afternoon, he decided to take her to the beach. So far everything was proceeding flawlessly. His house was a stone's throw away from the beach. He was trying to time everything to perfection. He was not an engineer for nothing.

Ten

Being a Sunday afternoon there was a fair crowd at the beach. The tide was high, and so the water lapped the sandy shore rhythmically, as it rose and waned faultlessly. It was not a perfect condition for swimming except for good swimmers. All others kept close to the shore careful not to risk being drawn into the deep water by the water current caused by the waves. There have been, on this very beach, incidents when even strong swimmers have been sucked into the deep waters and died unable to swim back to the shore. Close to the shore were many children with inflated tubes, who were learning how to swim under close watch of their teacher, while others played beach football on the sand. There were all manner of beach activities taking place including windsurfing. Both Jack and Claudia were greatly amused by a group of Asian women, who just sat in the shallow water fully clad in their saris, and chatted or meditated. Do women of any race and persuasion ever tire of talking? Jack silently mused. He could not tell about women, but the men he knew who spoke too much were either liars or conmen.

Claudia wanted to swim, but she had not brought her swimming gear. So she waded in the water to the knee level. Like a guard, Jack waited for her on the shoreline carrying her shoes.

"Why did you not swim in your clothes like those Asian women," Jack asked when she rejoined him after feeling satisfied with wading in the water.

"Because I feared you might find me funny."

"Would that matter as long as you have enjoyed yourself?"

"Still, I enjoyed myself while wading in the water. You don't have to swim to enjoy yourself. I assure you that next time I won't forget to bring my swimming suit."

"I too have enjoyed myself even though I didn't get into the water perhaps by just watching you. As you say I too will join you next time in the water."

"That will be more fun," she said enthusiastically.

"Can we pick a date for that?" Said Jack.

"Why not."

"Will next Sunday be fine with you?" He said speculatively.

"If it is with you."

"Then it is a date." They hugged each other for confirmation.

AFTER THAT, HE TOOK her to his fashionable flat. After conducting her around the house, they went and sat in his living room. He went to his music system and selected some music. Suddenly the room was filled with soothing soft music. He lived in the music world and could suffocate like a fish out of water away from music. He enjoyed all kinds of music. He felt like a prisoner at his place of work for lack of music.

He turned to Claudia and said: "I am famished. Can I make some sandwiches?"

Claudia said: "Let me come and help you."

They made some egg sandwiches took some beer from his fridge and carried them to the living room where they ate while listening to the music. After they had finished eating she turned to him and said: "Thank you for everything."

Nodding to her courteously he said: "It is my pleasure."

With their bellies quietened, they now listened to the music in earnest. After a while, she said: "You have a nice place here."

"It is not mine," he said modestly, "it belongs to the company. The only thing that belongs to me here is the music system"

"Wow," she said in surprise, "you are then taken very good care of by your company."

"All because we make them a lot of money. It is greasing the cog that drives the wheel."

She laughed because she did not know what else to say. However, his good music did not allow much conversation as they listened, their mind captured by it. No wonder the great English poet and playwright William Shakespeare quipped: "If music is food for the soul, then play it."

Nothing facilitates courtship more effectively than music. There was a time in his younger days, following the advice of his peers, when he would first take some alcohol before approaching a girl he wanted to court to get courage. Most of the time it did not work because once the girl realized he was drunk she doubted his sincerity or she did not like drunkards. His misguided peers had also advised him to memorize some magic verses, which if rendered to his prey, would leave her hopelessly in love with him. Trouble was when he met the target, he would be all nervous, and he would not recall the memorized verses. It had been all wasted time. And so intoxicated by the music, as it were, they did not notice the time fly until Claudia looked outside through the glass door, and realizing it was dark she exclaimed: "Jack! It's already dark. Please take me back to the hostel."

Her exclamation caught him by surprise, and he looked outside to confirm. All day long, he had been timing everything to perfection. It seemed finally his melodious music had somewhat dulled his sense of time. But he was not alarmed, so he said to her: "You could sleep here, and I will take you to work in the morning."

She said arising from her seat: "It would be too much of a hustle because I shall need to change my clothes. We can arrange when I can come prepared to sleep."

"When will it be convenient for you?" He asked her trying to hide his disappointment.

He had not expected a straight answer, and so he was surprised when she said: "Can you come and pick me up at my office on Wednesday?"

Had she already arranged this in her mind? Jack wondered before he promptly answered: "Of course." Can he ever say 'no' to a beautiful woman's request? He was incapable of that. It had caused him so much grief only yesterday, but today he could not remember it.

He did not like weekday dates because they interfered with his work, but for Claudia, he could do anything.

———◉———

AS HE DROVE HER BACK to her hostel, it was clear that the two had fallen in love with each other. It took them only one afternoon for that to happen. But would it last? However, everything has a beginning. Only time will reveal whether their love was a lasting one able to weather the storms of this world. At the parking lot of the hostel, he felt an urge to embrace her and kiss her but he restrained himself. He must be careful lest he frighten the bird and cause it to fly away, he successfully cautioned himself. She had the pedigree of the kind of wife he was seeking. He was satisfied by looking only at the outside. He knew his friends whose opinions he cared too much about would be impressed by his find. In his imprudence, he did not care how she might look inside. If he had heard the adage that all that glitter is not gold, he just ignored it.

His mind floated on cloud nine as he drove back to his house. He was the happiest man on earth, his happiness erasing from his mind the misery he had experienced with Mary and Susan only a day ago. How fast fortune can change? He mused. For that reason, he thought, it is never wise to lose hope. Tomorrow will be different from today. Nothing is permanent in this transient world. Be it joy or sorrow. St. Teresa of Avila put it so aptly: Let nothing frighten you, let nothing trouble you, everything passes away, whoever has God has everything. That means believing and trusting God, who created you and cares for you. This is a tall order for most people, including Jack. They erroneously assume that their lives are in their hands, which is far from the truth.

Eleven

As Jack impatiently waited for the appointed day, he thought of nothing else apart from Claudia. She was like a phantom that could not depart from his mind no matter how much he tried. Consequently, his work suffered due to a lack of concentration as he went about in a trance. However, the awaited day finally arrived. There was nothing peculiar about it in everybody else's eyes except his. The sun rose in its customary way and continued on its path in its usual pace even though he wished it was faster. Minutes before his work day ended he went to his boss and told him: "Sir, I want to leave work a little earlier today so that I can pick up a parcel at the post office before they close."

The boss lifted his eyes from his laptop and said: "Is that all Jack?"

"Yes, Sir," said Jack, wondering why his boss should ask him that.

"Ensure everything in your section is all right before you leave," his boss said.

"Yes, Sir," Jack said, much relieved.

As he closed the door of his boss's office, his keen eyes did not fail to see how his boss's eyes had gazed at him with concern. It was as though he knew that Jack was lying about the parcel. Had he noticed his laxity at work for the last few days? He must be careful no matter how much he felt about Claudia, he decided. Promotion to higher positions at work depended on one's performance. He wanted to climb up the corporate ladder as fast as he could. He was a man with a mission.

———◆———

WITHOUT MUCH TRAFFIC, he could get to Claudia's office in twenty minutes, but the evening traffic had started building up so that it took him half an hour to get to her office just in time for their closing.

The office block had three floors, but Claudia's office was on the ground floor. The offices were partitioned into small compartments with an aisle at the centre, the type you find in big firms. Apart from the receptionist compartment which was the first on your left as you entered the main door, all other compartments were occupied by typists/ secretaries. Claudia's compartment was opposite the receptionist's and she spotted Jack right away, as he entered because the partitions were of glass and you could see the entire office. She beckoned him to her partition.

"Hello Jack," she said smiling happily. "You have arrived at the very moment I have finished my day's work. It is perfect timing"

"It is good to see you, Claudia," Jack said to her also beaming, "I always keep time because I hate to keep people waiting."

She looked even prettier than before, perhaps because something was going on between them that radiated her face.

"Please take a seat as I go to the washroom to freshen myself."

"Thank you," he said stepping aside to let her pass.

From where he sat he surveyed the whole office. Most of the workers were women, he noted, some in their middle ages and a few youthful dressed to kill, and one or two men. He could not recognize any of them, which pleased him because these offices were rumour mills, and he did not want to jeopardize his relationship with Claudia in any way. Some of them stared in his direction, but he did not worry about them as long as he did not know any of them who might spread a rumour about them.

Claudia did not take long and as she was locking her door he said to her: "You people do not rush to go home when time is over."

"Whenever there is a lot of work, we try to clear as much as possible before going home to avoid clogging of work the following day." She explained, looking around to ensure she had not forgotten anything.

"I don't see much of that at my factory," he said modestly. "Most people watch the clock, and as soon time is over they leave everything to rush home as if there was an animal that might attack them if they lingered long after time is over."

"It is different here," she said indifferently.

"So I notice," he said, even though he could see she was not listening.

Twelve

He led her to his car and opened the door for her. She was elated because he had come to pick her up this time, and did not disappoint her as he did on the previous occasion. He too was very happy to be finally with her, as he switched on the ignition key, but to his chagrin, the car did not start. He tried again and again without success. Like a stubborn mule, it refused to respond. He sweated profusely, angry with the car. Claudia noted his dilemma and calmly asked him: "Is there something wrong with the car?"

He wiped the sweat from his face with a handkerchief and looking bewildered said: "I don't know why it can't start and I had no problem with it coming this way."

"Can I find a mechanic to have a look at it?" Claudia again asked as calmly as a hermit.

"Yes," he said, his face contorted with embarrassment. At that moment he wished the ground would open and swallow him. The happiness he had felt only a little while ago had suddenly turned into despair. How fast situations can change.

Barely five minutes and Claudia was back with a mechanic. "How are you, sir?" The mechanic said. "What is the problem with the car?"

"It can't start," Jack said despondently.

"Let's see," said the mechanic opening the hood of the car. He surveyed the engine meticulously, tightening any loose wire. Satisfied he told Jack: "Try it now."

With only one try the car burst into life. "There you are," said the mechanic smiling

"What did you do?" Asked Jack foolishly, his happiness returning.

"There was a loose wire which I tightened," the mechanic said casually.

Jack was an engineer, yet due to confusion caused by his embarrassment and concern about what Claudia might think of him, he did not even think of opening the hood to check for any apparent problem, as the mechanic did.

To mask his ignorance, he took his wallet, extracted a five hundred shillings note from it, and handed it to the mechanic saying: "Please take this for your trouble."

"Never mind sir," the mechanic said, shaking his head, "It was a very small problem."

"Please take it for your willingness to help," Jack insisted.

It was only when the mechanic turned to Claudia as if to seek her opinion and she nodded assent that he took the note saying to Jack: "Thank you so much, Sir."

"The pleasure is all mine," said Jack shaking his hand warmly.

ON THE WAY, HE ASKED Claudia: "What did you make of all that?"

"What do you mean by 'all that'?"

My car broke down when I came to pick you up as though some force was bent to embarrass me?"

"You are not superstitious, or are you?" She asked.

"Heavens no!" He protested vehemently.

"Then realize this: you can never escape problems in this world. The good news is that there are solutions to all problems."

He threw her a sideway glance amazed at her wisdom. He said, "You carry a wise head on your shoulders."

"It is common sense, Jack," she said smiling at him, "you had a problem and also its solution. It is the way of the world. Problems followed by solutions. If there were no problems in this world, it would be a very dull world indeed. The important thing is what we learn from the problem."

They carried on their discussion until they reached their destination, which was an exclusive beach hotel, not far from where he lived. It was already dark. The dining room which faced the ocean was dimly lit. The light from the hotel and its environs made the ocean water appear to glitter producing a surreal phenomenon. Jack marveled, at why the place looked so different at night than it looked during the day. At that time there was only a handful of other dinners. They sat at a corner table facing the ocean. They had a whole table to themselves.

"What will you have?" a waitress in a very smart uniform asked them courteously. They made their order and as they leisurely savoured their drink while they waited for the main course Jack brought back their previous discussion: "You said there is something we ought to learn from the problems we face. What do you think was the lesson of the problem we faced today, that of my car failing to start?"

"There are several lessons we can learn from that incident," she said: "the first one is you never panic. Face every problem calmly. If you do so you will be able to think clearly. Perhaps if you had been calm you might have thought of opening the hood of the car, and discover the loose wire. The second one is that we need each other to solve our problems. I helped in finding a mechanic, and the mechanic solved the problem."

"I will add the third lesson," Jack said laughing. "No one knows everything. I, as an engineer was today humbled by a mere mechanic. I will never forget that lesson."

"Hopefully it will make you a better engineer," Claudia said.

"Definitely," he said beaming.

By now they had finished their drinks and proceeded to the main meal. This time he was ready to pay for anything she requested.

Thirteen

They rested for a while after dinner before proceeding to the dancing hall. The resident band was excellent and played popular tunes flawlessly. Not only did both Jack and Claudia love to listen to music, but they also loved to dance, and so they danced until they were ready to drop. However, aware that the following day was a working day they left early and went to sleep at Jack's house. And from that day on they were ever together like Siamese twins. Their love for one another blossomed like that of Romeo and Juliet. However, it was not long before Jack came to appreciate the truth of what a famous singer once noted, when you are in love with a beautiful woman, you are in real trouble because every dude seems to want her or to snatch her from you. In the animal world, males establish their territory, by constant fights with rival males, ensuring no other male could touch their females. If another male challenges the owner of a territory the result is a fight, sometimes even to death or serious injury. Human beings are not different, sometimes they fight to death in defense of what they claim to be theirs. Sometimes, even close friendship is severed over suspicion that one friend is eyeing the sweetheart of the other friend. This is so prevalent, especially among the youth.

And so, whenever Jack and Claudia went to a social place it was customary for all eyes to follow them as if they were celebrities.

"Oh, those two are Kikuyus. You cannot tell by their appearance." Jack overheard one day from a lady in a group seated at a table next to theirs.

"Yes, the woman looks like a Seychellois, and the man as if he comes from western Kenya," another one responded.

Jack felt like screaming to them to mind their own business, but contrary to Jack, Claudia seemed to enjoy immensely the attention she received particularly from men. This infuriated Jack and he felt like beating up any man who dared even to stare at her. Why can't they see she was his? He fumed inside getting angry with Claudia. He felt so insecure and almost decided never to go with her to any social place. Still, he had no ground to suffer this insecurity because as far as he knew she showed no interest in anyone one else, and she passionately loved him. This insecurity robbed him of the Joy he would otherwise have enjoyed for finally finding the love of his life and could be detrimental to a healthy relationship devoid of any suspicion. And this insecurity did not start with Claudia. It was inherent in him like a disease. When he loved a woman, it was total love. He gave the relationship his all, which is unusual for men but common with women. This defect in him, for lack of a better term, manifested its ugly head in him when he got his first job after graduation from university. There was this young woman at his place of work with whom he fell in love with. She too fancied him. They dated for a while, and he even took her to his home one day to show her to his parents and also to let her know his home to confirm to her of his commitment. However, she was reluctant to introduce him to her parents as he had done. It was a clear signal that she was not that committed to their relationship, and in his naivety was not alarmed by it.

After some time, her feelings for him dwindled and she began to skip his dates. She did not like any of his friends and appeared uncomfortable whenever he was with them. Curiously, he noticed that most of her friends were women who preferred sugar daddies or sponsors as they were called. One day when he confronted her and asked her why she no longer kept his dates she told him she was not interested in poor young men. She was interested in real men who could offer her what she wanted. That hurt him because he loved her very much.

In his frustration, he drank and smoked more. He grew thin because he neglected eating for he had lost appetite for food. One day he overheard a woman he knew say to her friend: "See that Jack there, he has contracted a very serious disease. I cannot risk my health by shaking his hands."

The two crossed the road to avoid talking with him.

———◆———

ONE DAY, WHILE STILL languishing in his misery, he attended a friend's party in the company of a lass he had recently found to try to ease the agony slowly consuming him. He needed a woman to heal the injury caused by another woman. Heat is quenched by heat, he thought. But who should he find there in the company of a sugar daddy, than the very cause of his misery? Did she know he would be there and decided to come with her sugar daddy to spite him? He saw red, inducing him to drink more than what was good for him.

"Why can't your eyes leave that woman seated over there with another gentleman?" Asked the date he was with, puzzled by his behaviour and annoyed with him because he paid no attention to her or even danced with her.

"Let me go and see whether she is someone I know," he said rising up and wobbling drunkenly went to where the two were seated. He said: "Lydia, can I have a dance with you?"

"Don't you see that I am with somebody else?" She told him coldly, "Why can't you dance with the woman you are with?"

"I want to dance with you," he insisted.

"Please leave us alone Jack," she hissed at him, "I will not dance with you."

With his tail between his legs, as it were, he returned to his seat to face his now annoyed date.

"What type of a person you are?" She asked him.

He stared at her without answering her. He drank some more, his eyes never leaving Lydia.

"Did you come with me to mistreat me before all these people?" His date, fed up with him said.

"What do you mean," he stammered, "am I not with you?"

"But you are not interested in me, you seem more interested in the other woman," she said, almost in tears.

Paying no more attention to her he rose again saying: "Let me go and find out whether she is interested in me."

Fourteen

Lydia was at that moment dancing with her sugar daddy. He approached them and said to her: "Can I have a word with you?"

She turned to her date and said: "Let me take care of this nuisance once and for all."

She followed Jack to the door but before getting out she said: "Say whatever you want to say here where everyone can see us."

"We are not going far," he said, "it's just to keep away from the noise."

She stepped outside a few steps then stopped and said to him: " I will not go any further than here."

It will do, he thought and said: "Lydia, you know how much I love you. Why have you abandoned me and caused me all the suffering I am undergoing all because of my love for you?"

"If you are suffering," she said callously," that is your business. Deal with it. I told you I don't love you. I regret the time I wasted with you."

That stung him. He said painfully: "Why Lydia? Is it because I don't have a car or much money like the sugar daddy you're with?"

"Don't call my boyfriend a sugar daddy. Compared to him you're a mere boy. He is a man you can never hope to be even in the wildest of your dreams," she said contemptuously.

"Stop disrespecting me," Jack hissed at her, "else, I demonstrate to you what a man I am."

"Jack, are you a man, huh? What a joke of a man."

With that, he saw red and went for her throat. Petite she was, but strong as a bull, and because he had drunk too much, they both tumbled down to the ground his hands still on her throat like a vice, while her teeth like the incisors of a lioness were sunk into his forearm drawing blood.

Between gasps for air, she let out night-shattering screams that drew the happy dancers as well as the sugar daddy rushing out of the house to find out what was happening.

One of Jack's friends was the first to reach them and forcefully separate them. He said to Jack: "If a woman doesn't want you, why are you forcing her to want you?"

"I have not forced her to want me," said Jack defensively, ashamed to be accused by a friend.

"I have seen you with my own eyes," said his friend without backing down, "I have been watching you two."

Meanwhile, still screaming, Lydia continued to reign blows to Jack's head despite his friend's attempt to restrain her by getting between them. Even with short hands, she was very quick.

In the meantime, Lydia's boyfriend came out baying for Jack's blood but his friends prevented a physical fight between them.

"Let me fight him," yelled Jack, his eyes red, "to prove, before your eyes, who is the real man between him and me." He thought, with his youth, the man would not be a march to him but his friends would not allow it.

The man took Lydia's hand and led her to his car and they drove away, disappointed that what they had thought would be an enjoyable night had turned out nightmarish thanks to one Jack Karaya.

The owner of the party would not allow Jack back into the party, for the fracas he had caused, and he too fetched his date and shamefully left in a taxi, his hand painful from the bite inflicted by Lydia, the result of his folly.

"What happened to your arm Jack?" his father asked him, a few days later when he went home. He had not anticipated the question and urgently searched his mind for a suitable answer that would not reveal the real cause. He said, "My arm accidentally came into contact with a hot metal at work and got scorched."

"Uhhm...," his father said getting closer to examine the wound. He was not fooled, for his sharp eyes could identify teeth marks on the round wound. He said nothing but wondered why his son should lie to him. Had he fought with someone and did not want him to know? It was most probable. He worried too why he had lost so much weight. He loved him dearly, like the apple of his eye being his firstborn, and grieved that he had lied to him. He expected him to tell the truth, no matter what the problem was. He ought to have known, as his father, he would stand by him in all his problems. Had he failed in raising his children? He pondered in deep misery.

"He is encountering the challenges of life," his wife told him when he asked her later, whether she knew what was wrong with Jack.

"He is only a child, even though he has started working," she said.

That calmed him, but he said: "I think you're right, Mother. Indeed, boys will always be boys." They both burst into loud laughter. They were truly one body. In his life, Jack had never seen them fight. Their love for each other preached loudly to their children, making Jack seek a wife like his mother.

Fifteen

That was an incident Jack never wanted to remember. Whenever he met anyone who had been to that party he would cringe and avoid any discussion. That incident made Jack hate parties, and he kept away from them as much as possible.

That was how Jack was at this stage in his life. He competed with other young men for beautiful women, but his pride did not entertain possible rejection. It was common for most young men to fall in and out of love, as one breathes in and out, without any notable effect on them. It was not so with Jack. He did not know how to get out of a relationship. He was protective and detested those men who could not restrain their eyes from staring at his date.

Luckily he was not suicidal. There are many cases of youth, who after falling out with the one they love, lose hope and decide to end their lives. They forget that the sea is teeming with fish and a patient bird always gets a worm. There is someone for you, all according to God's plan.

After the debacle with Lydia, he thought he would never fall in love with any other woman again. The petite little Lydia, with teeth as sharp as those of a shark, had made him feel that way. However, after meeting Claudia, who was in a different league from Lydia in matters of elegance and beauty, he irrevocably changed his mind. But what had not changed, but went a notch higher was his insecurity and possessiveness. He fell in love hoping to be happy, but ended up miserable.

———◦———

CLAUDIA'S FATHER, PETER Mills, came to Kenya as an expatriate building instructor at a technical institution. He came to like the pleasant weather of the country in comparison to his native Britain, not least of all the amiable people. When his contract of five years ended, he chose to stay. By now he had met and married a local girl, Anne Wairimu, Claudia's mother after a painful divorce with his former English wife. He set up a building construction firm in the city amidst stiff competition. He had two daughters with Anne, the firstborn was named Pauline and then Claudia, separated by only two years. The parents were the directors of their firm. As they struggled to establish their firm, they chose to live in the cheaper part of Nairobi, commonly referred to as Eastlands. And so, for a while, their daughters went to school there. Later they transferred them to a boarding school upcountry where they thought they would get better education. To ensure they were always together, they enrolled them in the same class. Upon completion of their schooling, none of the girls had attained good enough grades to join university so they were enrolled in a two-year secretarial college to train as bilingual secretaries. On completion of their training, their father decided the elder, Pauline to join their firm to assist them in running it. They found a job for Claudia in a transport company. They continued to live with their parents even though they were now young women wanting to live an independent life.

One day, Claudia approached her mother and told her: "Mum, I find being a secretary such a drag. I want to do something else"

This startled her mother for she was her favourite daughter.

"Darling," her mother said gravely, "you have barely worked six months, which is a very short time to get to know your job well and probably come to like it."

Claudia said: "I don't think I will ever like it. Mom, it's a wrong career for me."

"What would you like to do?" Her mother asked.

She said: "I would like to be a model, I mean an international model such as Naomi Campbell and the rest."

"I don't know anything about modeling," her mother said in confusion, "to be able to offer you any advice, one way or another. I could say that you give your job more time just to get to know it well. Even if you become a model, who knows perhaps when you become old, and no longer fit as a model you may still have a career to fall back to."

She thought about what her mother said, then stated: "I accept what you say, mum. I'll give it a try but my heart is set for modeling."

"That's my girl," her mother said hugging her and feeling better.

Not long after that she was transferred to Mombasa and came to know, one Jack Karaya. Even though she continued to work as a secretary, her heart was truly in modeling and she knew she had what it takes to become a model.

For a model, someone's figure was critical, and she worked hard to keep her figure trim, caring for her hair meticulously, her nails, and her eyelashes. However, there was one critical thing that she forgot. She had sex freely with Jack and after three months she found out that she was pregnant. Angry with Jack, she faced him. They were in his house and Jack immediately realized something was wrong before she opened her mouth. He wondered whether she had had a bad day at work or what was wrong.

"How was your day?" He said, to bring up a conversation.

She was silent as though she had not heard his question, then without looking at him said: "I have been to see a doctor, and he said I am pregnant."

He looked sharply at her to ascertain she was not joking about such a serious matter. Satisfied she was not, he said: "In that case then, we must prepare ourselves to become parents, but first we must inform our parents."

"What do you mean, Jack? It seems pleasant news to you, while it's catastrophic for me." She said bitterly, staring at him, with strange hostile eyes, he had never seen before.

Flabbergasted, he said: "Why is it unwelcome news to you? Don't we love each other? Won't that make us love each other, even more? I don't understand you, Claudia."

"Yes, I love you Jack, and I know you can be a great husband," she said in desperation, "but it is too soon to get married. Besides, my father will kill me if he hears of it."

She was right that, although they were deeply in love, they had not had enough time to get to know each other well, to enter into a serious lifelong commitment. It waited for such a problem to surface to reveal their true identities.

He thought he had known Claudia well, but now it dawned on him that he had not. With not as many words he could sense what she was driving at. For him, there was no other solution except getting married.

Did she not confess that she loved him? As for him, he loved her more than he could love anyone. If they loved each other, then when the fruit of their love sprouts, what choice was there except getting married, whether her father wanted or not? She was not a minor and her father would do better than kill her and end up rotting in jail.

He asked her: "What do you want us to do?"

She looked at Jack and knew he would never agree to an abortion, and so her voice barely audible, she said: "Let this be a goodbye for each other."

His jaw dropped as though he had seen a ghost. It was a staggering blow to him. The ground swirled and he felt sick with nausea. The light in the room suddenly became dim, as though he was engulfed in immense darkness. He tried to think, but he was filled with confusion. After what seemed like an eternity, his face drenched in tears he asked her: "Why, Claudia?"

Without hesitation, she blurted out: "I have told you before, my goal in life is to become a model, and a model I shall be."

She was making it clear to him that she was pro-choice while he was pro-life. The two are anathema to each other. And that was what had formed her decision to call it quits.

Even though he was not a practicing Christian he held a strong view it was morally wrong to kill anyone let alone the unborn. They were people too.

He said to her: "What you are carrying is not your child, but our child."

"Yes, at the wrong time. I want first to be a model. Perhaps later I might become a mum."

"In life, you don't always get what you want."

"I'll try to get what I want. It is my body."

He remembered man was created by God, so he said: "No, it's not your body. You came from dust and to dust you shall return. If it was your body, you could refuse it to return to dust."

"As long as I am not dust yet, it is my body."

He said: "I will tell you what. Why don't you get the baby and become a model later?"

She said: "It doesn't work that way. My body will be damaged goods
"

He said: "Your body will never remain the same no matter what you do. In time it will change and grow old and finally die and cease to exist but if you have a child you will continue to live through the children ad infinitum. It is called regeneration."

She did not respond to his comment and he could see in her face that she was not interested in what he was saying.

That night she refused to sleep in his bed and slept in the extra bedroom. That night Jack did not sleep a wink. It puzzled him why she engaged in unprotected sex if she was afraid of getting pregnant. As for him he had no such worry for he was ready to marry her any day and have as many children as God will give them.

In his mind, Jack neither blamed Claudia nor exonerated himself. However, in the recesses of his mind, he could recall reading: "The Lord says: I call heaven and earth today to witness against you. I have set before you, life and death, the blessing and the curse, choose life." In a way, he was unconsciously obeying that command. It is peculiar that he was obeying this particular commandment while he disobeyed the others with impunity. He did not want a curse, either for himself or Claudia.

Even though it was Sunday she woke him before dawn. "Please take me to the hostel," she told him glumly.

They spoke not a word to each other, all the way to her hostel.

"Goodbye Jack," said Claudia, when she got out of the car, without looking at him or shaking his hand. It was as though she was fleeing from him.

He did not know what to say, so he just watched her hurriedly enter the hostel, as though in a hole. He remained sitting in the car wondering why everything turned grim for him in every woman he came to love. He felt what the prodigal son might have felt when he realized he had offended his father. It was true he had rejected God and disobeyed his commandments. He thought he was competent enough to run his life but had failed. He recalled Jesus' words: "Without me, you can do nothing."

For the first time instead of driving home, he found himself in the church compound just in time for the first mass. After mass, he spent an hour in the adoration chapel, gazing at Jesus and chanting: "Lord Jesus, have mercy on me a sinner."

It was strange he felt unusually calm when he got to his house. It was as though Christ had calmed the turbulent ocean of his life and breathed his peace into him. It was unmerited grace from God which he freely accepted. From that day his life took a different trajectory. When we encounter the person of Jesus Christ our life is never the same. Probably God was using these traumatic events in Jack's life to orchestrate a life of deep relationship with him in the future.

Sixteen

Like all women, Claudia enjoyed the attention showered to her by men, whenever she and Jack went to a social place. However, regardless of all the attention, she never wavered in her love for Jack because she saw how he loved her. She loved Jack more than any man she had known before she met Jack. Apart from her father, she had never experienced such love before. He was doting and self-giving. It is true, that other men ceaselessly approached her, but she never gave in to any of them. One day she told Jack: "I talked to Pauline today and she told me to greet you."

"Who is Pauline?" He asked her.

"My sister," she said.

"You have told her about me then?"

"Of course."

"In that case, I accept her greetings. Have you told your parents about us as well?"

"Not yet."

"And why not?"

"I will introduce you to them physically when we get ready." She said thoughtfully.

"I am ready now," he said breathlessly.

"Darling, you are so impatient," she rebuked him.

"I want to act when I have time for no one knows about tomorrow." He said enthusiastically.

"True, but too much haste spoils the broth."

"I don't know that. All I know is that I could take you to my parents tomorrow without viewing it as haste. An iron is hammered to the desired shape when hot."

"Doesn't the process commence by visiting the girl's parents?"

"Indeed, but you are not ready while I am."

"What do you think my parents will feel when they learn we have been to see your parents while they know nothing about it?"

"We will not have committed any crime," he said in exasperation.

Not reaching a consensus, they left the matter in abeyance but, continued to engage in unprotected sexual relationships unmindful of the consequences. And because they were healthy young people, what could happen, happened.

She became alarmed when she began having morning sickness. When it continued for a week she went and saw a doctor who conducted a test and confirmed her fears.

She walked wobbly from the clinic to the hostel room, escaping getting knocked by a car, as she crossed the road absent-mindedly.

That evening she went to Jack's house and told him. She saw her dream of becoming a model vanish into thin air. She blamed Jack for doing this to her. No, she will not allow this to happen to her. She called Pauline, her sister, who advised her to take leave from work and return home so that the two could plan the next move.

Seventeen

When Jack dropped Claudia at the hostel, she decided never to see him again. They used to call each other several times a day, but since that time whenever he called her, his line was blocked. He felt as though he was dreaming and hoped that when he woke up from the dream he would be relieved to discover that nothing wrong had happened between them, and they were still in love with each other as they had always been. When he called her office he was told she was on leave. He checked at her hostel but no one knew of her whereabouts. Where did she disappear to? He was greatly distressed and did not know what to do. Why was it that whenever he fell in love with someone he eventually ended up in grief? With Claudia, he had become certain that his search for a life partner had ended. He was both happy and content with her. All that remained were wedding preparations. And now see what has happened. Am I bewitched or what? He lamented as he slid into despondency.

He did not know to whom to turn to. His friends were not of any help. He took a long look at his miserable life. Why did his life not turn out the way he planned it? Why did he never accomplish his will no matter how meticulously he planned it? All these questions led to one answer. He had left God out of all his plans and most important of all his search for a life partner or what was God's plan for his life. What mission did God create him for? He made him for a purpose, what was it? He could not get the answers to these questions, in any other place apart from the Church. And so he shed off his old life, as a snake sheds off its skin, and returned to the Church.

⎯⎯◦⎯⎯

WHEN CLAUDIA ARRIVED in Nairobi she was met at the bus stop by Pauline. Apart from the weariness of the journey, she had no signs of pregnancy. The two sisters resembled one another except that Pauline was a shade darker.

"Not a word of this to our parents," Pauline said to Claudia. And so they swore to secrecy. Pauline had already consulted a private clinic, where the abortion would be done at an affordable cost. The parents were pleased to see their daughter and went about their business.

"You must be tired, eat something and go to sleep." Her mother said.

"I'll stay with her," Pauline said.

She knew better than not to argue with her, and so she joined her husband, and off they left for work.

"The doctor said it would not take more than two hours and then you'll be back to your former self," said Pauline assuring her.

"Oh, Pauline, I am so frightened," confessed Claudia.

"There's nothing to be frightened about, Claudia," Pauline said reassuringly, "girls are doing it all the time."

"Yes, but some of them die in the process." Said Claudia fearfully.

"Don't be silly Claudia," her sister reprimanded her sharply, "those who die go to quacks. I have booked for you a real doctor with an impeccable clinic."

"Oh, I wish I never got involved with Jack." Claudia moaned.

"It is too late for that, Claudia," said Pauline. "Let's get over this handle first, then we shall re-plan your future."

When this problem occurred, Claudia realized she could not get help to get rid of the pregnancy from Jack, her parents, or anyone else apart from her older sister Pauline, so she naively entrusted her life into Pauline's hands. And Pauline, on her part, was too eager not to help in saving the life of the innocent baby inside Claudia's womb, but her dream of becoming an international model by whatever means. Not once did Pauline give any thought to the innocent human being growing inside her sister's womb. It never occurred to her, that it was her sister's baby, and it had the right to life, no matter how tiny it was. If it occurred to her that it was a crime to both God and humanity, to kill anyone no matter how small one was, she repressed that thought, or as some people might put it, she buried her head in the sand, certain that no one will find out. And she planned the process to perfection.

THE FOLLOWING DAY THE parents were leaving for a business trip to Europe which was to take them two weeks, enough time to carry out their plans. The plan was that on the same day the parents left Claudia should enter the abortion clinic. By the time they returned from the overseas trip, Claudia should have recovered and probably returned to work in Mombasa.

There was no hitch in the plan and immediately the girls saw off their parents at the airport they went straight to the clinic. A nurse ushered them into the doctor's office.

"Please take a seat," the doctor said.

They nervously sat close to each other. To put them at ease the doctor said: "You resemble each other very much."

"We are sisters," Pauline said, "I am the eldest."

"Oh, I see," the doctor said beaming.

Claudia noted that the clinic was quite clean, still, it did not diminish her nervousness. Was she doing the right thing? She questioned herself. However, it was now too late to change her mind.

The doctor noticed her anxiety and said: "There's nothing to worry about Claudia. It is a simple procedure. Just relax. Claudia looked at her sister to draw strength from her. Seeing an encouraging smile from her sister she said to the doctor: "I am ready doctor."

The doctor said: "Your sister told me you want to make modeling your career. It is quite demanding for your body shape. Do you think you might want a child in the future or should we remove your uterus?"

She had not thought about that. She turned to consult her sister.

The doctor said: "Go to that room and discuss the matter. When you have decided come and tell me."

When they were alone Claudia nervously asked Pauline: "What do you think sis.?"

"To have or not to have children, is a personal decision, Claudia. If you're set on making modeling your career, by the time you decide to retire from that career, you might be forty or fifty, which will be too late to have children. In any case, you can always adopt a child. The decision must be yours, and you must tell the doctor, not me." Pauline said.

"I have made a decision," Claudia said resolutely.

When they returned to the doctor's office he asked Claudia: "Have you made a decision?"

There was a deafening silence. It was not only the doctor who was anxious to know what she had decided, so too was Pauline. They both stared at her with their breaths abated as she opened her mouth and said: Yes, doctor. I have made a decision "

In unison, as though by a common voice, the doctor and Pauline asked: "What is it?"

This startled Claudia, who hesitated momentarily before she said in an almost inaudible voice: "Remove the uterus."

"Are you sure?" Again in unison both Pauline and the doctor asked.

"Yes, I am." Replied Claudia emphatically.

Pauline gasped. She looked at her sister and repeated: "You are sure?"

Claudia said: "Yes, I am sure, Pauline. I have never been surer."

Pauline turned to the doctor and said: "You have heard from the horse's mouth "

"Yes, I have Pauline. You can leave her with me now. After the procedure, she will need rest and observation. Please come to see her in the evening around six." The doctor said.

Pauline hugged her sister and said: "Everything will be all right sis. Don't be afraid."

Both of them smiled at each other affectionately, and Pauline left.

⸺⬤⸺

THE DOCTOR AND PAULINE were wrong to make Claudia make such a critical decision in her state of mind. At that time, she needed counseling and more time to make an informed decision.

On her way home Pauline worried. What if something went wrong? What would their parents think of her? She did not want to think about it but the thought would not go away.

Eighteen

Pauline was greatly relieved to find Claudia alive and in bed, wearing off the effects of asthenia, when she returned to the clinic in the evening to see her. Two days later she was discharged and went home. As days passed, her physical body seemed to recover from the effects of abortion, but her mental health seemed to ail, deteriorating with each passing day. She developed mood swings. One moment she is very happy and in the next, she would flip into a deep depression. It was as though there were two people sharing her body. One happy, the other sad. The duration of each state varied unpredictably.

When she was on the happiness swing, she talked of nothing else, other than how Jack was a good loving man and how the two loved each other. On the sadness swing she talked of the mistake she made of aborting their son, she was positive it was a son and feared that neither Jack nor God would forgive her for that crime.

At night she screamed and screamed, alleging that the ghost of the aborted baby was attacking her. Other nights she laughed and laughed the night away.

Alarmed by her condition, and fearful that their parents might return home and discover what had happened, Pauline took her to a psychiatrist who prescribed some drugs for her which somehow calmed her. However, she was not at peace regretting her role in this Claudia's affair. Things had not turned out the way she had hoped.

A few days before their parents returned, Claudia had relatively recovered, and Pauline had gone to work. Without informing anyone, Claudia took a Mombasa-bound bus which she knew would drop her near Jack's house.

At around five in the morning, she knocked at Jack's door.

"Who is it?" Jack asked, wondering who it was who was waking him up at such an hour.

There was no answer, so he asked for a second time: "Who is it?"

There was some shuffling of feet from outside, then a voice he could never mistake anywhere gently announced: "It's I, Claudia."

Jack's heart almost missed a beat when he heard her voice.

"One minute," he shouted from his bedroom, and covering himself decently rushed to open the door.

Under the glow of the security light, she looked more beautiful and elegant than he could ever remember. He noticed that she had no luggage whatsoever, not even a handbag. She was only with the clothes she was in. In a cheerful voice, he said to her: "Please come in."

He led her to the living room she knew too well and both of them sat down. Still sleepy and yawning, he said to her: "Oh Claudia, I am so happy to see you. Where did you disappear to? I have looked for you everywhere."

She stared at him, as though to confirm it was really him before she said, her eyes shining: "I have come back to you, darling. Never mind where I went to."

He was not reassured, instead, he was alarmed by her appearance at his door with nothing, as though she had dropped from outer space. He said to her: "Can I make you something to eat?"

She said: "Perhaps something to drink."

He went to the kitchen and came back with a can of Coke and a glass. She gulped it thirstily.

"Some more?" He asked her when she put the glass down on the coffee table.

"Yes please," she said expectantly.

He rose again and went back to the kitchen and came back with another can of coke. This time she drank it slowly.

"Where have you come from at this time of night?" Jack asked her when she had finished drinking.

"I have come from Nairobi. I felt I needed to come over and ask for your forgiveness for what I did," she said.

It did not make sense to Jack, but he said: "If you have come from Nairobi you must be very tired. Why don't you rest now then you can tell me what you want to tell me later?"

When she did not say anything, he led her to the spare bedroom and told her: "I want you to rest, meanwhile I will report to work, later I will come so that you can tell me everything. If you need anything to eat you know where to find it."

"Thank you," she said, and he closed the door behind him.

He came back at around eleven in the morning. The door was unlocked but she was not in the house. Where could she have gone to? he wondered. Perhaps she had gone to the beach, he thought, and waited for her. He waited for a while and then decided to return to work hoping that she would be back by the time he came back from work in the evening.

Nineteen

Now that she had seen Jack and asked for his forgiveness, Claudia urgently needed to complete her mission. She no longer felt any fatigue as she walked five kilometers to the centre of the Nyali bridge. On the bridge, people went to and fro without anyone paying attention to her. The traffic zoomed past her unabated. She hesitated briefly gazing at the bluish sea water twenty or so meters below. But she had made up her mind and there was no turning back. She saw some fishermen leisurely rowing a canoe not far from the bridge but paid no attention to them. As though to defy the world by welcoming her death, she momentarily hung on the rails and took her last breath, before plunging into the dark sea below.

And thus beautiful and elegant Claudia ended her life. She felt that deep waters could not quench her love for Jack, nor floods sweep it away. Alas, how short was her life on this earth? Where will her soul be upon leaving her body? She was created for eternal happiness with God in heaven. Did her ambition to become an international model deceptively lead her to lose everything, especially the perfect bliss her heart craved?

A loud splash below the bridge attracted the fishermen and some passersby, but no one knew with any certainty what had happened. However, some News stations reported that someone had jumped or had been pushed into the sea from the bridge. Nobody could tell how they got the story, but it elicited swift action from the authorities.

The Navy was called and it took their divers a whole day to recover the already bloated body and take it to the mortuary.

———◉———

A WEEK OR SO LATER Jack received a phone call from the C.I.D. office in Mombasa asking him to report to their office immediately. He was gripped by fear. What could be the reason for him to be summoned there? He worried. He was particularly apprehensive because C.I.D. officers had a reputation for torturing people, and even some people had disappeared for good while in their custody. He had now returned to Church, and as it had become his custom he went to the adoration chapel in their parish and prostrated himself before the Lord Jesus, asking for his protection and guidance. "Don't be afraid. I am with you." He heard him say that, and it melted his fear away making him ready and willing to meet the C.I.D. officers.

He drove himself calmly to the C.I.D. offices and upon introducing himself he was led to the interrogation room.

As he entered the room he made the sign of the cross and interiorly prayed: "Our Father....In your hands, I place my soul...Hail Mary..."

He felt immense peace descend upon him. He knew that the Holy Spirit would give him the necessary answers to their questions.

There were three Police officers in civilian clothes, their desks arranged in a U-formation with a chair at the centre, where he was ordered to sit. All three officers could see any movement or expression on his face. One of them had a tape recorder before him.

The one at the centre, who appeared to be their senior said to Jack: "Tell us your name and what you do for a living."

Calmly Jack replied: "My name is Jackson Karaya. I am an engineer at the Rip milling factory."

"As an engineer, you must be a very busy person at your factory," said the officer on his left, "we will not take much of your time."

The senior officer introduced himself and the others, then said: "We are investigating the disappearance of a certain lady by the name of Claudia Mills. We believe you might have information that could help us. Do you know her?"

At the mention of Claudia's name, his face froze with fear. My God, where did she vanish from my house? For a minute or so he was speechless. He cried out to the Lord, "Help me."

He was there beside him. Re-discovering his composure he said: "I know her. We had a relationship that lasted for about six months. She broke our relationship and returned to Nairobi, only to reappear at my doorstep at 5 am last Wednesday. She told me she had come to ask for my forgiveness. Since I didn't have much time as I was going to work I told her to rest and wait until I returned. When I returned I found the door open but she was not there. I don't know where she disappeared to. What I can say is that she appeared to be in mental anguish, but I didn't have enough time with her to properly establish what she was suffering from."

The officers consulted each other and told him to go outside for a while until they called him back.

When he was outside they called his office to confirm what he had said and his record. They said he was at work on that Wednesday and that his character was impeccable.

When he was called back into the interrogation room, the senior officer told him: "There is a dead body of a woman which was retrieved from the sea at Nyali bridge. We want to take you to the mortuary to see whether you can tell us whether she is the one."

On hearing that he fainted and slumped in his chair. He would have slid to the ground had not one of the officers quickly grabbed him. After about half an hour he was sufficiently recovered.

One of the officers asked him: "Can you identify her?"

His voice hardly audible said: "Yes."

He looked half-dead and had to be supported to the mortuary, a journey that took no more than ten minutes.

At the mortuary, he was certain she was the one.

"How can you tell?" The police officer asked him.

"I know her face anywhere, whether dead or alive."

When they returned to the office, the three policemen wearing dark goggles stared at him curiously, without saying a word. None of them saw any need to ask him further questions. Then the senior officer in a commanding voice said: "You can go."

"Praise the Lord!" Jack shouted exuberantly. He did not doubt that God had been with him and protected him from the legendary callousness of the C.I.D. officers. He could not believe that he had escaped from their hands unscathed. And why had he at one stage panicked and forgot that the faithful Lord had told him not to fear? He attributed this to his little faith and asked God to increase his faith.

He marveled why God snatched him from the lion's jaws, as it were, considering how a great sinner he was. It must be out of his great love for him and he felt truly grateful. How could he repay him for that? He remembered our Lord saying: 'Repent and believe in the gospel ' He prayed that God may fill him with grace, as he did to our Blessed Mother, so that he may never sin again and thus offend God.

⬥

UNKNOWN TO JACK, CLAUDIA'S parents had been summoned to Mombasa and had conclusively identified the body.

In Nairobi, Pauline had confessed everything, and she and the abortion doctor had been arraigned in court to face the full force of the law. Pauline had correctly guessed that Claudia might have travelled to Mombasa to see Jack. That was why the C.I.D. summoned him.

That incident turned Jack's life upside down. He thought of his beloved Claudia, possessed by the desire to be a model at any cost. Would she have found fulfillment after becoming a model? How long would that fulfillment have lasted?

He remembered the Scripture which says: "*Unless the Lord builds the house, they labour in vain who build. Unless the Lord guards the city, the guards keep watch in vain.*

That was what Claudia was doing. Building her future. What about himself? Was he not doing the same thing when he was trying too hard to get married? Did he ever think of God's plan for his life? Just like Claudia he craved fame, status, happiness, and security. He indeed had a good job but he lacked lasting peace and happiness which money could not buy.

The event also reminded him of the demoniac from whom Jesus cast out two thousand unclean spirits. Upon leaving the demoniac, the demons entered a herd of swine which plunged into the sea, and drowned. He wondered whether an unclean spirit had left the abortion demoniac, and entered into Claudia driving her to plunge into the sea and drown. A demon always causes death and we have to be watchful for demoniacs, such as that of abortion, and others that are sprawling around us ready to spring and kill.

⸻⬤⸻

THE CONGLOMERATES OF the recent events surrounding his life inspired Jack to take a hard long look at his life. He asked himself, why did God create him? Why was he so good to him in spite of his unfaithfulness to him? God called, shouted, and broke through his deafness.

Returning to the Church brought God close to him. He no longer doubted his existence. He was amazed by his great love for him despite his sinfulness. He felt so indebted to him. He learned that God created him to know him, to love him, to serve him, and finally to be with him in heaven, which means to be his family. Can anything be more awesome than that? All his life he had unknowingly distanced himself from God. Still, God was always beside him, protecting him and providing his needs, and never giving up on him.

Created things kept him from him. Now he wanted to correct that by first finding out what was his will for him. What had he planned for his life? Did God call him for a married life in view of his many failed attempts? To get these answers he spent many hours lying prostrate before the Blessed Sacrament in the adoration chapel at his parish imploringly God for discernment. After months of this accompanied by fasting, he felt God was calling him to serve him in the priesthood.

Concluding that the decision could no longer be delayed, he went to see the vocations director of his diocese.

After the preliminary introduction he said to the priest: "Father, I feel called into the priesthood.

The short plumb priest studied him for a while before asking him: "Why? Is it because you can't get someone to get married to?"

Jack was staggered by the priest's bluntness, but looking at him straight in the face he said: "No, I don't think so Father. Yes, I have made several attempts to get married, and failed, breaking my heart miserably but that is not the reason I want to become a priest. Yes, I didn't get married, Father, simply because that was not what God willed."

"What is the reason, then?" The priest asked curiously.

"Because, Father," Jack said a little animated, " I want to serve God, I want to bring people to him, I want people to know him. I want people not to be the way I was."

The priest looked flabbergasted. He had not met someone for a while with such passion. Nevertheless, he arranged several sessions with him just to make sure he meant what he said before enrolling him in the seminary.

Jack resigned from his employment, to leave everything and follow Jesus in the footsteps of the apostles.

Don't miss out!

Visit the website below and you can sign up to receive emails whenever Francis Kiarie publishes a new book. There's no charge and no obligation.

https://books2read.com/r/B-A-HVCCB-HGEEF

BOOKS 2 READ

Connecting independent readers to independent writers.

About the Author

After a brief stint as a teacher in a secondary technical school, he joined the cement manufacturing industry where he worked for close to twenty years. Since retirement, he has now engaged in farming, business, and writing.